FROM DARKNESS TO LIGHT: THE RESILIENCE OF LIFE IN THE UNIVERSE

DISCOVERING THE WONDERS OF THE UNIVERSE AND LEARNING TO LIVE IN HARMONY WITH THEM.

ANYAGWA KENNETH

Made with ♥ on the Notion Press Platform
www.notionpress.com

DEDICATION

To all the curious minds who have ever looked up at the night sky and wondered about the mysteries of the universe.

To the scientists and researchers who have dedicated their lives to exploring the world around us and making groundbreaking discoveries.

To the environmental activists and advocates who are working tirelessly to protect our planet and ensure a sustainable future for all.

And finally, to my family, friends, and loved ones who have supported me on this journey of discovery and encouraged me to pursue my passion for science and the natural world.

This book is dedicated to all of you. May we continue to marvel at the wonders of the universe and work together to ensure a bright and sustainable future for ourselves and future generations.

Contents

Foreword

FOREWARD

It is with great pleasure that I introduce this book on the fascinating story of how the world was formed. The author, Anyagwa Kenneth, has spent a lifetime studying the wonders of the universe and the natural world and brings a wealth of knowledge and insight to this topic.

In this book, Kenneth takes us on a journey through time and space, exploring the origins of the universe and the forces that shaped our world. He covers a vast array of topics, including the Big Bang theory, the formation of stars and galaxies, the evolution of life on Earth, and the various threats that face our planet today.

What makes this book particularly compelling is Kenneth's ability to make complex scientific concepts accessible and engaging to a general audience. He has a gift for storytelling and a passion for the natural world that shines through on every page.

This book is not only an exploration of the mysteries of the universe, but also a call to action. Kenneth reminds us that the fate of our planet is in our hands and that we have the power to make a difference in the world.

I highly recommend this book to anyone who is curious about the world around them and wants to learn more about the fascinating story of how the world came to be. It is an inspiring and thought-provoking read that will leave you with a newfound appreciation for the wonders of the universe and the resilience of life

Preface

PREFACE

In the course of human history, we have been fascinated by the mysteries of the universe and the world around us. We have marveled at the wonders of the natural world, sought to understand the forces that govern our world, and pondered the ultimate questions of existence.

This book is the result of a lifelong fascination with the universe and the natural world. It is an attempt to explore the fascinating story of how the world came to be, from its earliest beginnings to the present day.

In this book, we will delve into the history of our world, exploring the many theories and discoveries that have helped us piece together the story of our planet. We will examine the various forces that shaped our world, from the birth of the universe to the evolution of life on Earth. We will also look at the threats that face our planet today and the steps we can take to ensure a brighter future for ourselves and future generations.

It is my hope that this book will serve as an inspiration for readers to continue exploring the mysteries of the universe and to appreciate the resilience of life in the face of adversity. I believe that the story of the world is one that is worth telling, and I hope that you will join me on this journey of discovery

Acknowledgements

ACKNOWLEDGEMENT

First and foremost, I would like to thank my family for their unwavering love and encouragement throughout this journey. Your support has meant everything to me.

I would also like to thank my friends and colleagues who have offered their feedback, support, and encouragement along the way. Your insights and perspectives have been invaluable.

I am deeply grateful to the scientific community for their tireless efforts in exploring the mysteries of the universe and the natural world. Your work has inspired and informed much of the content in this book.

Finally, I would like to express my appreciation to my readers. Without your curiosity and thirst for knowledge, this book would not exist. I hope that this work will inspire you to continue exploring the wonders of the universe and to appreciate the resilience of life in the face of adversity

Prologue

PROLOGUE

The universe is vast and mysterious, filled with wonders that have captivated the imaginations of people for centuries. We have gazed upon the stars and wondered about their origins, marveled at the complexity and diversity of life on Earth, and pondered the ultimate questions of existence.

From the earliest creation myths to the most cutting-edge scientific discoveries, humans have sought to understand the origins and workings of the cosmos. We have developed complex theories, models, and technologies to help us unravel the mysteries of the universe, but we are still only scratching the surface.

In this book, we will embark on a journey through time and space, exploring the fascinating story of how the world came to be. From the birth of the universe to the formation of our planet, we will delve into the history of our world and the forces that shaped it.

We will explore the various theories and discoveries that have helped us piece together the story of our world, from the Big Bang theory to the evolution of life on Earth. We will also examine the threats that face our planet today and the steps we can take to ensure a brighter future for ourselves and future generations.

This book is a celebration of the human spirit of curiosity and exploration, a tribute to the wonders of the universe and the resilience of life. So join me on this adventure, as we journey through the vast expanse of space

and time, exploring the mysteries and beauty of the world we call home

From Darkness to Light: The Resilience of Life in the Universe

Discovering the Wonders of the Universe and Learning to Live in Harmony with Them.

Once upon a time, the universe was nothing more than a vast expanse of darkness, with nothing to be seen but a handful of twinkling stars. Amid this darkness, however, something remarkable was happening.

In the heart of the universe, a tiny spark of energy began to glow, slowly growing brighter and brighter until it exploded with a great burst of light. The explosion created a vast cloud of gas and dust, which began to swirl and spin in space, gradually forming the first galaxies and stars.

As the universe expanded and evolved, new planets and moons were born, including the beautiful blue and green sphere we call Earth. For billions of years, this planet thrived, teeming with life in all its forms, from tiny microbes to towering dinosaurs.

But then, something began to change. Humans, the most advanced and intelligent species on the planet, began to take over. They cut down forests, polluted the air and water, and caused irreversible damage to the delicate ecosystems that supported life on Earth.

From Darkness to Light: The Resilience of Life in the Universe

Despite the warnings of scientists and environmentalists, humans continued on this path, driven by greed and short-sightedness. They thought only of their own immediate needs and desires, ignoring the long-term consequences of their actions.

As the years passed, the damage grew worse and worse. The climate changed, the oceans warmed, and the ice caps melted, leading to catastrophic storms, floods, and droughts. Species after species went extinct, unable to survive in the changing environment.

Finally, it seemed that there was nothing left to save. The planet was dying, and there was no hope for a future.

But then, a strange thing happened. Amid the chaos and destruction, a small group of humans came together. They were scientists, engineers, and environmentalists, and they had a bold and daring plan.

From Darkness to Light: The Resilience of Life in the Universe

Using the latest technology and their collective knowledge, they set out to create a new world, one that would be free from the mistakes of the past. They worked tirelessly, day and night, pouring all their efforts into the project.

And finally, after years of hard work, they succeeded. A new world was born, one that was clean, pristine, and perfect in every way. It was a world that was free from the damage caused by humanity, a world that was a haven for life in all its forms.

But then, just as they thought they had succeeded, something went wrong. A small group of humans had survived the destruction of the old world, and they were determined to take over the new one.

They attacked the scientists and engineers, destroying their work and taking control of the new world. They took everything that they wanted, using it for their selfish purposes, ignoring the consequences of their actions.

And so, once again, the world was doomed. The new world, free from the mistakes of the past, was destroyed by the same old greed and ignorance that had caused so much damage before.

From Darkness to Light: The Resilience of Life in the Universe

In the end, there was nothing left but darkness, a vast expanse of nothingness that stretched out into infinity. The universe was once again empty, with a handful of twinkling stars, a reminder of what had been lost.

As the universe was plunged back into darkness, a glimmer of hope began to shine. It came from an unlikely source, a small band of humans who had survived the destruction of the old world and the downfall of the new.

These humans, unlike their predecessors, were filled with a deep sense of humility and respect for the natural world. They had been able to survive by living in harmony with their surroundings, learning from the lessons of the past, and making a conscious effort to live sustainably.

As they gazed out at the darkness of the universe, they were filled with a sense of wonder and awe. They realized that they were part of something much larger than themselves and that they had a responsibility to care for the world around them.

So they embarked on an adventure that would take them to the ends of the universe. They traveled through galaxies and star systems, encountering strange and wondrous creatures along the way.

From Darkness to Light: The Resilience of Life in the Universe

They learned from these creatures, studying their behavior and how they interacted with their environment. They were inspired by the beauty and diversity of the universe, and they resolved to do everything in their power to protect it.

Slowly but surely, the humans began to make a difference. They worked tirelessly, developing new technologies and solutions to the challenges they faced. They planted forests and restored damaged ecosystems, working to reverse the damage caused by previous generations.

As they worked, they began to see the fruits of their labor. The skies cleared, the oceans became clean, and the land was once again filled with life. The world began to thrive once more, a testament to the resilience of life in the face of adversity.

And so, the humans continued on their journey, inspired by the beauty and wonder of the universe. They knew that there would be challenges ahead, but they were ready to face them head-on, confident in their ability to overcome any obstacle.

In the end, the universe was filled with light once more, a shining beacon of hope for all those who called it home. The humans had learned from their mistakes, and they had worked hard to make amends for the damage they had caused.

As they looked out at the vast expanse of space, they knew that much work was still to be done. But they were ready, armed with the knowledge and determination to create a brighter, better future for themselves and all the creatures of the universe.

9 798889 756965

Printed by Libri Plureos GmbH in Hamburg,
Germany